Deuce — A catcher holds down two fingers to tell the pitcher to throw a curve. *Deuce* means "two," thus deuce is a curveball.

Dinger — A home run.

Dish — Home plate.

Ducks on the Pond — Runners on the bases, waiting to be driven home.

Fat Pitch — A pitch that is easy to hit.

Goat — A player whose error loses an important game.

Grand Slam — A home run hit with a runner on every base.

Green Light — A signal given to a batter that tells him he can swing at the next ball if he chooses.

Gun — A pitcher's arm that is exceptionally strong and capable of throwing a bullet-fast pitch.

Hit the Dirt — Said of a player when he slides into a base, also of a batter who falls down in order to avoid being hit by a pitch.

Jughandle — A curveball, called this because its path resembles the shape of a jug's handle.

Take Me Out to the Ball Game

From *Take Me Out to the Ball Game*
Words by Jack Norworth
Music by Albert Von Tilzer

FRANK and ERNEST PLAY BALL

by Alexandra Day

Green Tiger Press ~ MMXI

Dedicated, with thanks, to Satchel, The Big Train, The Say Hey Kid,
The Georgia Peach, Old Aches and Pains, The Rajah,
Dizzy and Dazzy, The Rabbit, Pie, The Splendid Splinter,
Big and Little Poison, Yogi, The Wizard of Oz, The Babe,
Big 6, The Vulture, Gabby, The Gray Eagle, The Bird,
Blue Moon, The Yankee Clipper, The Iron Horse,
and all the others.

THIS IS A REPRINT OF A BOOK ORIGINALLY PUBLISHED IN 1990
by SCHOLASTIC INC.

GREEN TIGER PRESS
A DIVISION OF LAUGHING ELEPHANT
LAUGHINGELEPHANT.COM

Library of Congress Cataloging-in-Publication Data

Day, Alexandra.
Frank and Ernest play ball / by Alexandra Day. -- Reprint ed. p. cm.
Summary: With the help of a baseball dictionary so they can learn the necessary language,
an elephant and a bear take over the management of a baseball team.
ISBN 978-1-59583-438-6
[1. Elephants--Fiction. 2. Bears--Fiction. 3. Baseball--Fiction.] I. Title.
PZ7.D32915Fs 2011
[E]--dc22
2010048046

"I need someone to take care of my baseball team, the Elmville Mudcats. I've never been away from it before, during the season, but my wife has planned a 25th-anniversary trip to our old hometown, and I can't disappoint her. It will be a hard job because I do almost everything for my team, but it will be for only one game."

"We like challenges, Mr. Palmer. We don't know much about baseball, but we'll work hard at learning. I'm sure everything will be all right."

Elmville is a very small town, but we have many fine fans. I'm sure you will enjoy yourselves."

"This job sounds like fun, but we should find out what we can about it before we start."

"Here's *The Dictionary of Baseball*. I think this will be very helpful. Is there anything you want me to look up, Ernest?"

"See if it tells what they use all of the fans for."

"Yes, here it is."

pitch thrown when the
danger of walking a batter;
hrows a pitch that is easy

ffee — A minor-league
y brief opportunity to play
r leagues.

A catcher holds down two
tell the pitcher to throw a
ce means "two," thus deuce
all.

— A home run.

Home plate.

n the Pond — Runners on the
aiting to be driven home.

Fans — Enthusiastic supporters of a sports team. It may be a shortened form of *fanatic*, a person who is a wild and excessive adherent to a cause.

Farm — The system of minor-league teams that supplies players to the big leagues.

Field General — A team's mana

Fireman — A pitcher who is b into a game to take over for a p who is not doing well.

Flake — A player who acts in a str manner, on or off the field.

Fly Hawk — A skilled outfielder, w moves toward the ball he must catc like a hawk to its prey.

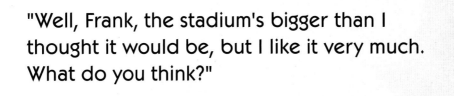

"Well, Frank, the stadium's bigger than I thought it would be, but I like it very much. What do you think?"

"I wonder why the Mudcats are in a cellar!"

"Let's check the *Dictionary* and see what it says."

Cellar — The team in last place in a baseball league is said to be in the cellar because it is at the bottom, as a cellar is beneath a house.

Frank & Ernest—
These are the
jobs you will
need to do
while I'm gone.
Good luck!
~ Joe Palmer

EVERYDAY ACTIVITIES
ELMVILLE MUDCATS

1. Prepare the field: Cut and water the grass. Rake the dirt part of the infield. Remake the chalk lines.

2. Count the money. Start selling the tickets. (Be sure to count the money again at the end of the day.)

3. Help with batting practice.

4. Help with fielding practice.

5. Turn on the floodlights

6. Help take the rest of the tickets from all the people who come in just before the game begins.

7. Take over the job of radio announcer. Describe the game to the fans at home.

8. When the game concludes, open all the gates for the fans to go out.

9. Turn off the lights and lock the gates.

"I think we'd better get busy with our jobs, Frank."

"I guess if we eat our lunch on the field we'll have to be careful about pepper."

"Let's look up pepper in the *Dictionary* and see why it is bad for baseball."

"I left the book in the ticket booth, so we can look it up when we go to sell tickets."

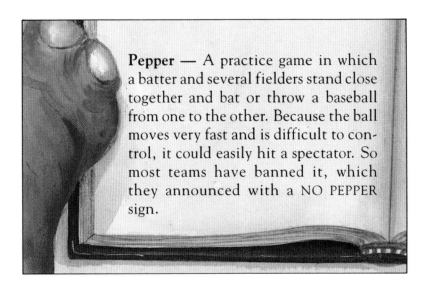

Pepper — A practice game in which a batter and several fielders stand close together and bat or throw a baseball from one to the other. Because the ball moves very fast and is difficult to control, it could easily hit a spectator. So most teams have banned it, which they announced with a NO PEPPER sign.

"Can I help you, sir?"

"Let me have a ticket as near to the hot corner as possible."

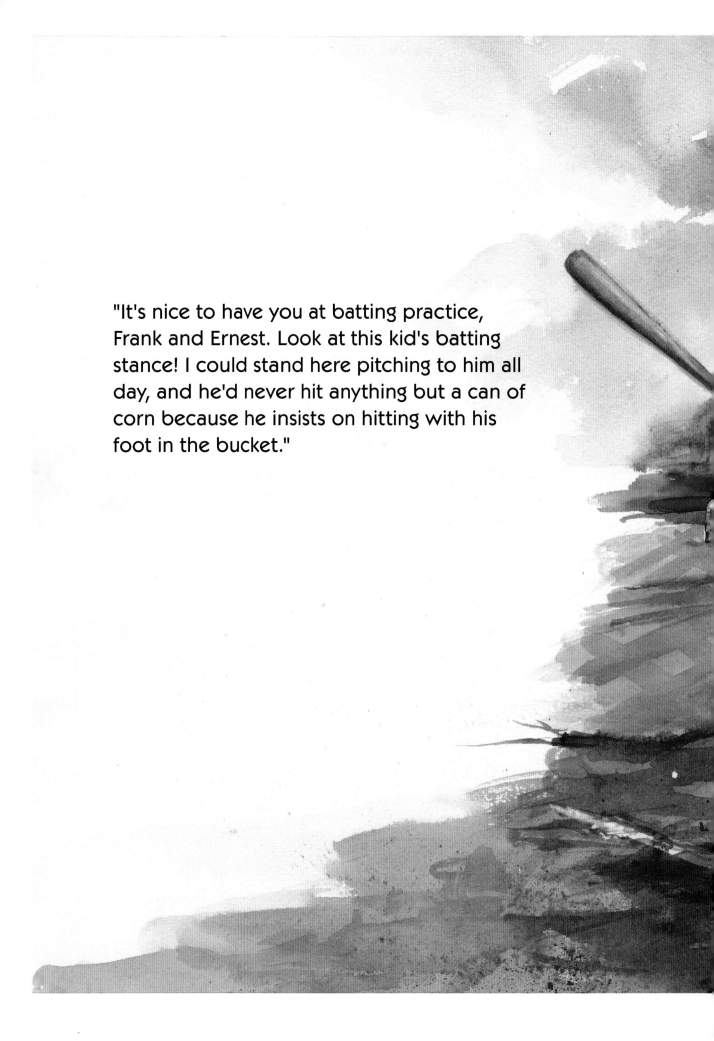

"It's nice to have you at batting practice, Frank and Ernest. Look at this kid's batting stance! I could stand here pitching to him all day, and he'd never hit anything but a can of corn because he insists on hitting with his foot in the bucket."

Can of Corn — A fly ball that can easily be caught. Bob Prince, the Pittsburgh Pirates' announcer, would often say, "It's as easy as taking corn out of a can."

Foot in the Bucket — A hitter who moves his front foot sideways, and away from home plate, as he swings at the ball is said to hit with his foot in the bucket.

"I'll bet you've never seen a fungo bat before, Frank and Ernest. It's thinner and lighter than a regular bat, and we use it to hit balls to the fielders during practice."

"Here come the people to see the game, Frank."

◆◆◆◆

"I hear they've got the meal ticket pitching."

"He has a rubber arm."

"I hope that butterfingers isn't playing right field."

"They could win if they had a better bullpen."

"That was some rhubarb Tuesday night."

"That kid Harris is a hot dog, but I like him."

"I thought we understood most of what we needed to know, Ernest, but the longer we're here, the more things I realize there are to learn."

The Meal Ticket — A team's best pitcher, the one they can count on for a good performance.

A Rubber Arm — A pitcher who has a strong and resilient arm.

Butterfingers — A fielder who drops a ball. The term comes from the idea that balls slip through his fingers as if the fingers had been buttered.

Bullpen — The group of pitchers who stand ready to relieve the starting pitcher if he needs help; the area just outside the playing field where pitchers warm up their arms during a game.

Rhubarb — A noisy, active argument between players on opposing teams.

Hot Dog — A player who goes out of his way to draw the fans' attention to himself during the game.

"Let's keep the book in front of us while we broadcast, Ernest. We'll be able to look up all the terms as we need them."

"Tonight the Mudcats' starting pitcher is Charlie Bennett, a left-handed pitcher who throws heat. The Beavers' pitcher is Jim White, a right-handed smoke artist."

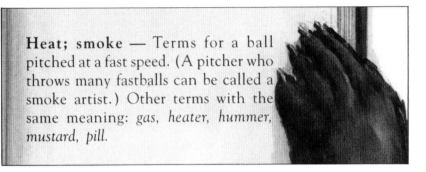

Heat; smoke — Terms for a ball pitched at a fast speed. (A pitcher who throws many fastballs can be called a smoke artist.) Other terms with the same meaning: *gas, heater, hummer, mustard, pill.*

"Agnes Martin, from right here in Elmville,
will sing the National Anthem for us tonight."

"Oh, say can you see by the dawn's early light
What so proudly we hailed at the twilight's
    last gleaming?
Whose broad stripes and bright stars through
    the perilous fight,
O'er the ramparts we watched were so
    gallantly streaming?
And the rocket's red glare, the bombs
    bursting in air,
Gave proof through the night that our flag
    was still there.
Oh, say does that star-spangled banner
    yet wave
O'er the land of the free, and the home of
    the brave?"

"Marshall hits the first pitch high in the air, and Brady, our fly hawk, makes the catch."

Fly Hawk — A skilled out-fielder, who moves toward the ball he must catch like a hawk to its prey.

"Bennett gave two Beavers free transportation this inning, but kept them both from scoring."

ELMVILLE

	1	2	3	4	5	6	7	8	9	10		R	H	E
BEAVERS	0	0	0									0	1	0
MUDCATS	0	0										0	1	0

AT BAT	BALL	STRIKE	OUT
7	2	1	1

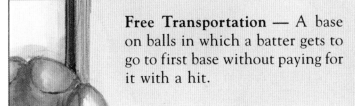

Free Transportation — A base on balls in which a batter gets to go to first base without paying for it with a hit.

ELMVILLE

	1	2	3	4	5	6	7	8	9	10	R	H	E
BEAVERS	0	0	0	0	0	0					0	1	0
MUDCATS	0	0	0	0	0	1					1	2	0

AT BAT	BALL	STRIKE	OUT
31	3	1	2

"That's a frozen rope from home plate into the stands for the first run of the game."

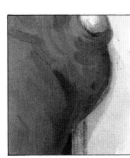

Frozen Rope — A ball is hit so hard that it follows a path as straight as a stretched rope. Also called a *rope*, a *blue darter*, or a *screaming meemie*.

"He's out at home, which wins the game for the Mudcats, who move out of the cellar on their way to the top."

ELMVILLE
1 2 3 4 5 6 7 8 9 10
R H E
BEAVERS
MUDCATS
AT BAT
BALL
STRIKE
OUT

"Well, Frank, that was a wonderful experience. I'm going to miss the Mudcats."

"Me, too! Now that we're baseball fans, we can go often to see games played."

"Yes, we will, and let's always sit near the hot corner."

Juice — To hit the ball a long way.

K — In keeping score, this letter stands for a strikeout. It was chosen because it is the last letter of *struck*.

Lumber — A bat. A team with many powerful hitters is said to have a lot of lumber.

Payoff Pitch — The pitch delivered with three balls and two strikes on the batter.

Phenom — A young player who is expected to be a star. It is taken from the word *phenomenon*.

Punch and Judy Hitter — A batter who specializes in softly struck, but successful, hits.

Rabbit Ears — A player, or umpire, who is easily offended by others' remarks is said to have rabbit ears.

Rag Arm — A player who throws without success.

Scroogie — A short form of *screwball,* a pitch that breaks in the opposite direction from a curveball.

Sent to the Showers — What happens to a pitcher who is pitching badly and has to be removed from the game.